# *Flower Fairies of the Trees*

POEMS AND PICTURES BY

CICELY MARY BARKER

D1187065

BLACKIE: LONDON AND GLASGOW

## LOOK UP!

Look up, look up, at any tree!
There is so much for eyes to see:
Twigs, catkins, blossoms; and the blue
Of sky, most lovely, peeping through
Between the leaves, some large, some small,
Some green, some gold before their fall;
Fruits you can pick; fruits out of reach;
And little birds with twittering speech;
And, if you're quick enough, maybe
A laughing fairy in the tree!

Distributed in the United States by
Two Continents Publishing Group Ltd.,
30 East 42nd Street, New York, NY10017

*copyright*
*All rights reserved*

Blackie & Son Ltd., Bishopbriggs, Glasgow
450 Edgware Road, London W2 1EG

*Printed in Great Britain by Smith and Ritchie Ltd., Edinburgh.*

# CONTENTS


| | |
|---|---|
| Almond Blossom | 4 |
| Box Tree | 6 |
| Blackthorn | 8 |
| Pear Blossom | 10 |
| Wild Cherry Blossom | 12 |
| Lilac | 14 |
| Beech Tree | 16 |
| Laburnum | 18 |
| Guelder Rose | 20 |
| Elder | 22 |
| Sycamore | 24 |
| Lime Tree | 26 |
| Cherry Tree | 28 |
| Poplar | 30 |
| Mulberry | 32 |
| Ash Tree | 34 |
| Willow | 36 |
| Pine Tree | 38 |
| Elm Tree | 40 |
| Alder | 42 |
| Sweet Chestnut | 44 |
| Silver Birch | 46 |
| Plane Tree | 48 |
| Christmas Tree | 50 |
| Botanical names | 52 |

## ALMOND BLOSSOM

Joy! the Winter's nearly gone!
Soon will Spring come dancing on;
And, before her, here dance I,
Pink like sunrise in the sky.
Other lovely things will follow;
Soon will cuckoo come, and swallow;
Birds will sing and buds will burst,
But the Almond is the first!

*The Almond Blossom Fairy*

## BOX TREE

Have you seen the Box unclipped,
Never shaped and never snipped?
Often it's a garden hedge,
Just a narrow little edge;
Or in funny shapes it's cut,
And it's very pretty; *but*—

*But*, unclipped, it is a tree,
Growing as it likes to be;
And it has its blossoms too;
Tiny buds, the Winter through,
Wait to open in the Spring
In a scented yellow ring.

And among its leaves there play
Little blue-tits, brisk and gay.

*The Box Tree Fairy*

## BLACKTHORN

The wind is cold, the Spring seems long
a-waking;
The woods are brown and bare;
Yet this is March: soon April will be making
All things most sweet and fair.

See, even now, in hedge and thicket tangled,
One brave and cheering sight:
The leafless branches of the Blackthorn,
spangled
With starry blossoms white!

(The cold days of March are sometimes called "Blackthorn Winter".)

*The Blackthorn Fairy*

## PEAR BLOSSOM

Sing, sing, sing, you blackbirds!
  Sing, you beautiful thrush!
It's Spring, Spring, Spring; so sing, sing, sing,
  From dawn till the stars say " hush ".

See, see, see the blossom
  On the Pear Tree shining white!
It will fall like snow, but the pears will grow
  For people's and birds' delight.

Build, build, build, you chaffinch;
  Build, you robin and wren,
A safe warm nest where your eggs may rest;
  Then sit, sit, sit, little hen!

*The Pear Blossom Fairy*

## WILD CHERRY BLOSSOM

In April when the woodland ways
  Are all made glad and sweet
With primroses and violets
  New-opened at your feet,
    Look up and see
      A fairy tree,
    With blossoms white
      In clusters light,
All set on stalks so slender,
  With pinky leaves so tender.
O Cherry tree, wild Cherry tree!
  You lovely, lovely thing to see!

*The Wild Cherry Blossom Fairy*

## LILAC

White May is flowering,
  Red May beside;
Laburnum is showering
  Gold far and wide;
But *I* sing of Lilac,
  The dearly loved Lilac,
Lilac, in Maytime
  A joy and a pride!

I love her so much
  That I never can tell
If she's sweeter to look at,
  Or sweeter to smell.

*The Lilac Fairy*

## BEECH TREE

The trunks of Beeches are smooth and grey,
  Like tall straight pillars of stone
In great Cathedrals where people pray;
  Yet from tiny things they've grown.
About their roots is the moss; and wide
  Their branches spread, and high;
It seems to us, on the earth who bide,
  That their heads are in the sky.

And when Spring is here, and their leaves appear,
  With a silky fringe on each,
Nothing is seen so new and green
  As the new young green of Beech.
O the great grey Beech is young, is young,
  When, dangling soft and small,
Round balls of bloom from its twigs are hung
  And the sun shines over all.

*The Beech Tree Fairy*

## LABURNUM

All Laburnum's
Yellow flowers
Hanging thick
In happy showers,—
Look at them!
The reason's plain
Why folks call them
" Golden Rain "!
" Golden Chains "
They call them too,
Swinging there
Against the blue.

(After the flowers, the Laburnum has pods with what look like tiny green peas in them; but it is best not to play with them, and they must never, never be eaten, as they are poisonous.)

*The Laburnum Fairy*

## GUELDER ROSE

There are two little trees:
In the garden there grows
The one with the snowballs;
All children love *those*!

The other small tree
Not everyone knows,
With her blossoms spread flat—
Yet they're both Guelder Rose!

But the garden Guelder has nothing
When her beautiful balls are shed;
While in Autumn her wild little sister
Bears berries of ruby red!

*The Guelder Rose Fairies*

## ELDER

When the days have grown in length,
When the sun has greater power,
Shining in his noonday strength;
When the Elder Tree's in flower;
When each shady kind of place
By the stream and up the lane
Shows its mass of creamy lace—
Summer's really come again!

*The Elder Flower Fairy*

## SYCAMORE

Because my seeds have wings, you know,
  They fly away to earth;
And where they fall, why, there they grow—
  New Sycamores have birth!
Perhaps a score? Oh, hundreds more!
  Too many, people say!
And yet to me it's fun to see
  My winged seeds fly away.
(But first they must turn ripe and brown,
  And lose their flush of red;
And *then* they'll all go twirling down
  To earth, to find a bed.)

*The Sycamore Fairy*

## LIME TREE

Bees! bees! come to the trees
Where the Lime has hung her treasures;
Come, come, hover and hum;
Come and enjoy your pleasures!
The feast is ready, the guests are bidden;
Under the petals the honey is hidden;
Like pearls shine the drops of sweetness
there,
And the scent of the Lime-flowers fills the air,
But soon these blossoms pretty and pale
Will all be gone; and the leaf-like sail
Will bear the little round fruits away;
So bees! bees! come while you may!

*The Lime Tree Fairy*

## CHERRY TREE

Cherries, a treat for the blackbirds;
  Cherries for girls and boys;
And there's never an elf in the treetops
  But cherries are what he enjoys!

Cherries in garden and orchard,
  Ripe and red in the sun;
And the merriest elf in the treetops
  Is the fortunate Cherry-tree one!

*The Cherry Tree Fairy*

## POPLAR

White fluff is drifting like snow round our feet;
Puff! it goes blowing
Away down the street.

Where does it come from? Look up and see!
There, from the Poplar!
Yes, from that tree!

Tassels of silky white fluffiness there
Hang among leaves
All a-shake in the air.

Fairies, you well may guess, use it to stuff
Pillows and cushions,
And play with it—puff!

(This is called the Black Poplar; but only, I think, because there is also a White Poplar, which has white leaves. The very tall thin Poplar is the Lombardy.)

*The Poplar Fairy*

## MULBERRY

"*Here we go round the Mulberry bush!*"
You remember the rhyme—oh yes!
But which of you know
How Mulberries grow
On the slender branches, drooping low?
Not many of you, I guess.

*Someone* goes round the Mulberry bush
When nobody's there to see;
He takes the best
And he leaves the rest,
From top to toe like a Mulberry drest:
This fat little fairy's he!

*The Mulberry Fairy*

## ASH TREE

Trunk and branches are smooth and grey;
(Ash-grey, my honey!)
The buds of the Ash-tree, black are they;
(And the days are long and sunny.)

The leaves make patterns against the sky,
(Blue sky, my honey!)
And the keys in bunches hang on high;
(To call them "keys" is funny!)

Each with its seed, the keys hang there,
(Still there, my honey!)
When the leaves are gone and the woods are bare;
(Short days may yet be sunny.)

*The Ash Tree Fairy*

## WILLOW

By the peaceful stream or the shady pool
I dip my leaves in the water cool.

Over the water I lean all day,
Where the sticklebacks and the minnows
play.

I dance, I dance, when the breezes blow,
And dip my toes in the stream below.

*The Willow Fairy*

## PINE TREE

A tall, tall tree is the Pine tree,
  With its trunk of bright red-brown—
The red of the merry squirrels
  Who go scampering up and down.

There are cones on the tall, tall Pine tree,
  With its needles sharp and green;
Small seeds in the cones are hidden,
  And they ripen there unseen.

The elves play games with the squirrels
  At the top of the tall, tall tree,
Throwing cones for the squirrels to nibble—
  I wish I were there to see!

*The Pine Tree Fairy*

## ELM TREE

Soft and brown in Winter-time,
Dark and green in Summer's prime,
All their leaves a yellow haze
In the pleasant Autumn days—
See the lines of Elm trees stand
Keeping watch through all the land
Over lanes, and crops, and cows,
And the fields where Dobbin ploughs.
All day long, with listening ears,
Sits the Elm-tree Elf, and hears
Distant bell, and bleat, and bark,
Whistling boy, and singing lark.
Often on the topmost boughs
Many a rook has built a house;
Evening comes; and overhead,
Cawing, home they fly to bed.

*The Elm Fairy*

## ALDER

By the lake or river-side
  Where the Alders dwell,
In the Autumn may be spied
Baby catkins; cones beside—
  Old and new as well.
Seasons come and seasons go:
  That's the tale they tell!

After Autumn, Winter's cold
  Leads us to the Spring;
And, before the leaves unfold,
On the Alder you'll behold,
  Crimson catkins swing!
They are making ready now:
  That's the song I sing!

*The Alder Fairy*

## SWEET CHESTNUT

Chestnuts, sweet Chestnuts,
  To pick up and eat,
Or keep until Winter,
  When, hot, they're a treat!

Like hedgehogs, their shells
  Are prickly outside;
But silky within,
  Where the little nuts hide,

Till the shell is split open,
  And, shiny and fat,
The Chestnut appears;
  Says the Fairy: "How's *that*?"

*The Sweet Chestnut Fairy*

## SILVER BIRCH

There's a gentle tree with a satiny bark,
All silver-white, and upon it, dark,
Is many a crosswise line and mark—
She's a tree there's no mistaking!
The Birch is this light and lovely tree,
And as light and lovely still is she
When the Summer's time has come to flee,
As she was at Spring's awaking.

She has new Birch-catkins, small and tight,
Though the old ones scatter and take their flight,
And the little leaves, all yellow and bright,
In the autumn winds are shaking.
And with fluttering wings and hands that cling,
The fairies play and the fairies swing
On the fine thin twigs, that will toss and spring
With never a fear of breaking.

*The Silver Birch Fairy*

## PLANE TREE

You will not find him in the wood,
    Nor in the country lane;
But in the city's parks and streets
    You'll see the Plane.

O turn your eyes from pavements grey,
    And look you up instead,
To where the Plane tree's pretty balls
    Hang overhead!

When he has shed his golden leaves,
    His balls will yet remain,
To deck the tree until the Spring
    Comes back again!

(Besides the balls, which turn to brown silky fluff in the Spring, and fly away, you may know the Plane by its strange peeling bark, in piebald patches of dark and light grey.)

*The Plane Tree Fairy*

## CHRISTMAS TREE

The little Christmas Tree was born
  And dwelt in open air;
It did not guess how bright a dress
  Some day its boughs would wear;
Brown cones were all, it thought, a tall
  And grown-up Fir would bear.

O little Fir! your forest home
  Is far and far away;
And here indoors these boughs of yours
  With coloured balls are gay,
With candle-light, and tinsel bright,
  For this is Christmas Day!

A dolly-fairy stands on top,
  Till children sleep; then she
(A live one now!) from bough to bough
  Goes gliding silently.
O magic sight, this joyous night!
  O laden, sparkling tree!

*The Christmas Tree Fairy*

## BOTANICAL NAMES

The botanical names are those in use at the Royal Botanic Gardens, Kew.

| ENGLISH NAME | BOTANICAL NAME | NATURAL ORDER |
|---|---|---|
| Almond | *Prunus Amygdalus* | Rosaceæ |
| Box | *Buxus sempervirens* | Euphorbiaceæ |
| Blackthorn (or Sloe) | *Prunus spinosa* | Rosaceæ |
| Pear | *Pyrus communis* | Rosaceæ |
| Wild Cherry (or Gean) | *Prunus avium* | Rosaceæ |
| Lilac | *Syringa vulgaris* | Oleaceæ |
| Beech | *Fagus sylvatica* | Fagaceæ |
| Laburnum | *Laburnum Anagyroides* | Leguminosæ |
| Guelder Rose (wild) | *Viburnum Opulus* | Caprifoliaceæ |
| Guelder Rose (Snowball) | *Viburnum Opulus, var. sterile* | Caprifoliaceæ |
| Elder | *Sambucus nigra* | Caprifoliaceæ |
| Sycamore (Great Maple; Scottish Plane) | *Acer pseudoplatanus* | Aceraceæ |
| Lime (or Linden) | *Tilia vulgaris* | Tiliaceæ |
| Cherry (cultivated) | *Prunus avium* | Rosaceæ |
| Poplar (Black) | *Populus nigra* | Salicaceæ |
| Mulberry | *Morus nigra* | Moraceæ |
| Ash | *Fraxinus excelsior* | Oleaceæ |
| Willow (Crack Willow or Withy) | *Salix fragilis* | Salicaceæ |
| Pine (Scots) | *Pinus sylvestris* | Coniferæ |
| Elm (common) | *Ulmus procera* | Ulmaceæ |
| Alder | *Alnus glutinosa* | Betulaceæ |
| Sweet (or Spanish) Chestnut | *Castanea sativa* | Corylaceæ |
| Silver Birch | *Betula pendula* | Betulaceæ |
| Plane (London) | *Platanus acerifolia* | Platanaceæ |
| Christmas Tree (Spruce Fir) | *Picea Abies* | Coniferæ |

Some very familiar trees will be missed from this book: the Apple, Oak, Hazel, Horse Chestnut, Larch, Hawthorn, Mountain Ash, Holly, and other trees. This is because they appear in other books of the Flower Fairy series.